Text copyright © 2020 by Nikki Tate • Illustrations copyright © 2020 by Katie Kath
All Rights Reserved • HOLIDAY HOUSE is registered in the U.S. Patent and Trademark Office.
Printed and bound in November 2019 at Tien Wah Press, Johor Bahru, Johor, Malaysia.
The artwork was created with watercolor and pastel. • www.holidayhouse.com
First Edition • 1 3 5 7 9 10 8 6 4 2
Library of Congress Cataloging-in-Publication Data
Names: Tate, Nikki, 1962- author. | Kath, Katie, illustrator. | Title: Home base : a mother-daughter story/by
Nikki Tate ; illustrated by Katie Kath. | Description: First edition. | New York : Holiday House, [2020]
Summary: "A gutsy baseball-playing girl and her bricklaying mom celebrate when love and hard work triumph
over nerves"— Provided by publisher. | Summary: In interwoven narratives, a young girl and her mother support
one another as one tries out for the baseball team and the other interviews for a bricklaying job, then celebrate
their success together. | Identifiers: LCCN 2019003118
ISBN 9780823436637 (hardcover) | Subjects: CYAC:
Mothers and daughters—Fiction. | Determination
(Personality trait)—Fiction. | Baseball—Fiction.
Bricklaying—Fiction. • Classification: LCC PZ7.
T211275 Hom 2020 • DDC [E]—dc23 • LC record
available at https://lccn.loc.gov/2019003118

Home Base

A Mother-Daughter Story

by NIKKI TATE   illustrated by KATIE KATH

HOLIDAY HOUSE
NEW YORK

Cereal.
Bananas.
Milk.

Tryouts.
Fitness?
Skills?
Experience?

Cap. Glove. Shoes.

Gloves. Goggles. Boots.

Ball.
Bat.
Base.

String line.
Chalk.
Mallet.
Trowel.

Ballpark.
Dirt mound.
Base.

Bubblegum.

Catch.
Toss.
Grin.

Job site.
Wheelbarrow.
Oozing mortar.

Butter.
Scrape.
Smooth.

Homework.
Chores.
Long day.

Bills.
Dinner.
So tired.

Imagine.
Dream.
Sleep.

Plan.
Rest.
Snooze.

Solid stance.
Step in.

Measure twice.
Organize.

Straight. Fast.

Strike three! Out!
Way to go! We won!

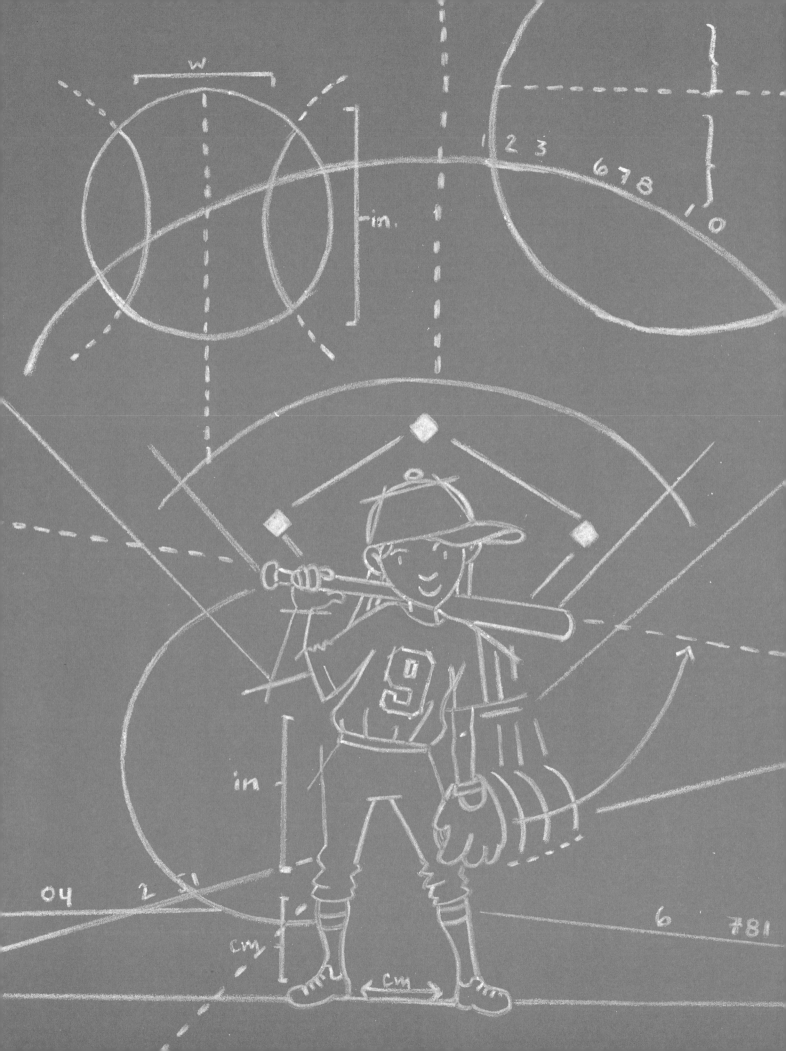